Illustrated by
the Disney Storybook Art Team

A GOLDEN BOOK • NEW YORK

rhcbooks.com

ISBN 978-0-7364-4344-9 (trade)

Printed in the United States of America

10 9 8 7 6 5 4 3 2 1

Somewhere in the depths of outer space, a Star Command ship nicknamed the Turnip detected valuable resources on a remote planet. Captain **Buzz Lightyear** and his fellow Space Ranger, Commander **Alisha Hawthorne**, went to explore the surface. Suddenly, **vines** came to life and a **swarm of giant bugs** dove toward them.

"Back to the Turnip!" Alisha ordered.

Once on board the ship, Alisha hurried back to the engine room to make sure that the ship's engines had enough power to launch.

Buzz raced to the cockpit, jumping into one of the two pilot's seats. He worked both control wheels to make sure the ship cleared the mountain range that was rapidly approaching, **but the bottom of the ship scraped against the big rocks**.

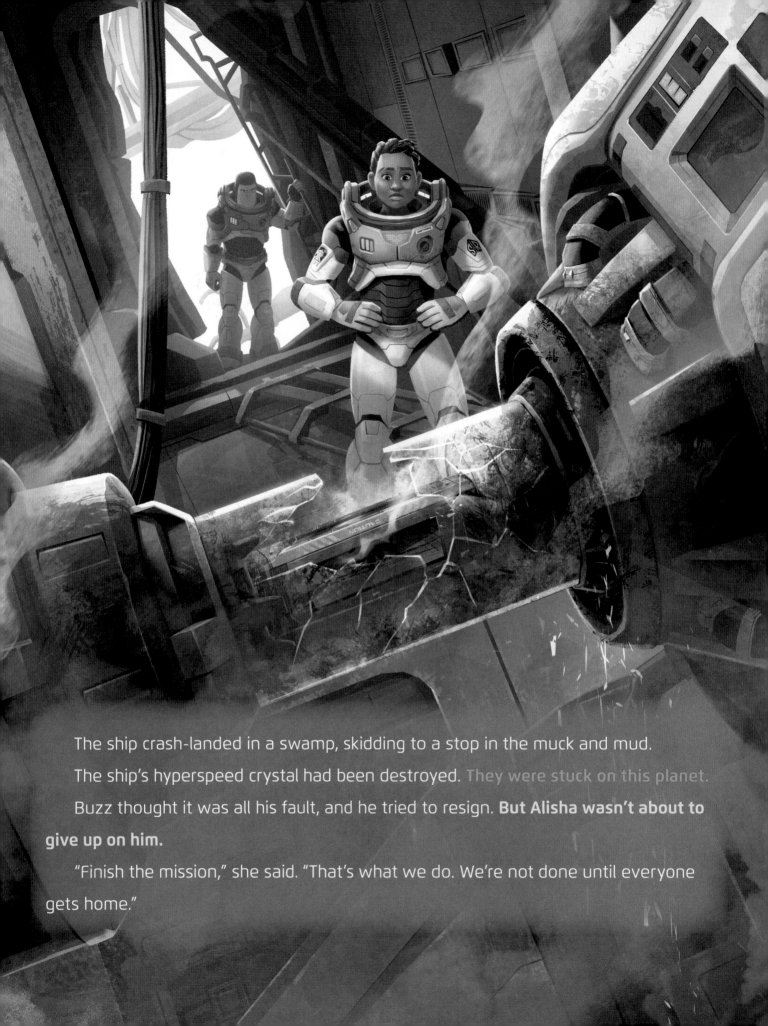

The ship crash-landed in a swamp, skidding to a stop in the muck and mud.

The ship's hyperspeed crystal had been destroyed. They were stuck on this planet.

Buzz thought it was all his fault, and he tried to resign. **But Alisha wasn't about to give up on him.**

"Finish the mission," she said. "That's what we do. We're not done until everyone gets home."

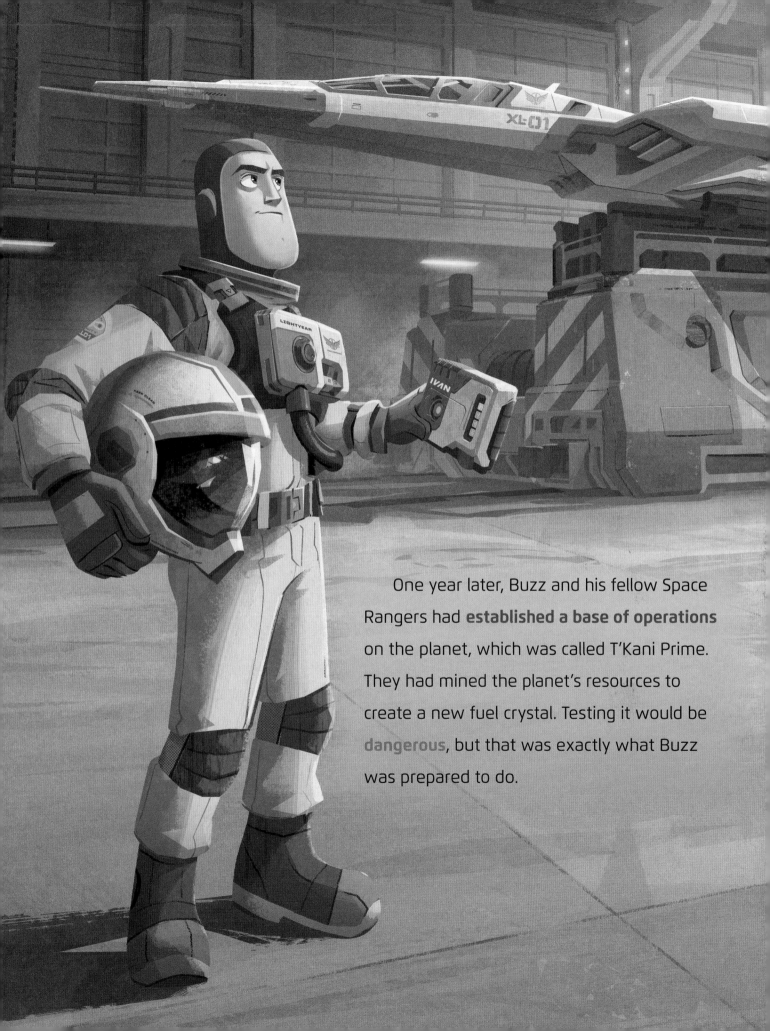

One year later, Buzz and his fellow Space Rangers had **established a base of operations** on the planet, which was called T'Kani Prime. They had mined the planet's resources to create a new fuel crystal. Testing it would be **dangerous**, but that was exactly what Buzz was prepared to do.

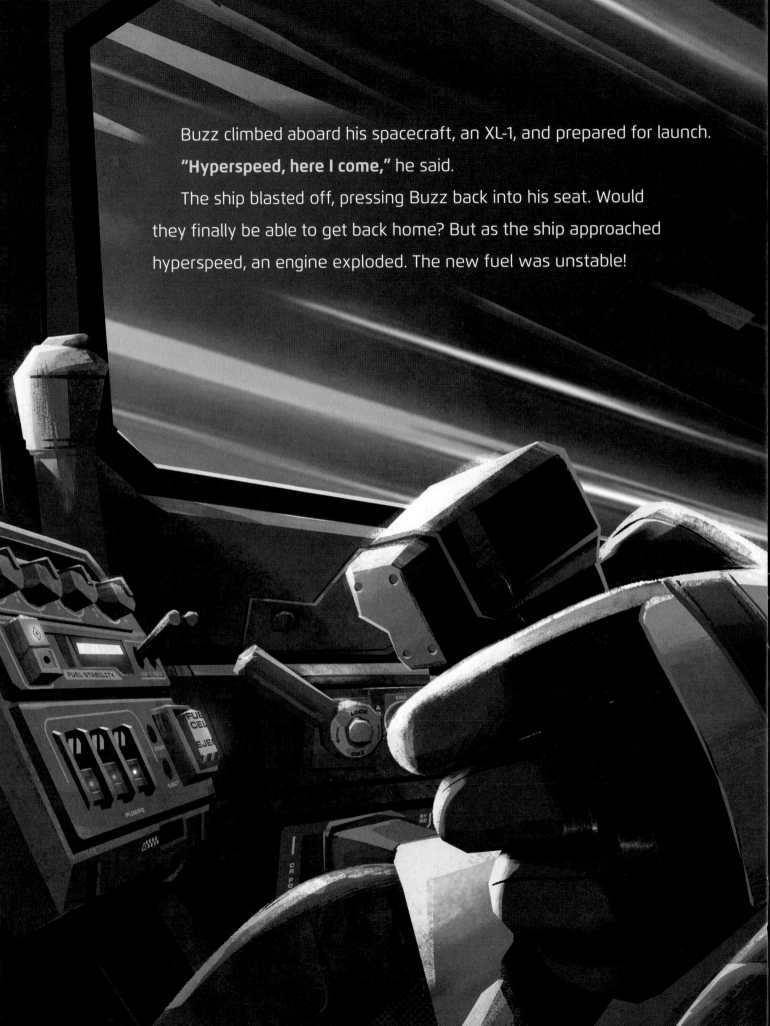

Buzz climbed aboard his spacecraft, an XL-1, and prepared for launch.
"Hyperspeed, here I come," he said.

The ship blasted off, pressing Buzz back into his seat. Would they finally be able to get back home? But as the ship approached hyperspeed, an engine exploded. The new fuel was unstable!

After landing the XL-1, Buzz learned that **four years, two months, and three days** had passed. How was that possible?

"Time dilation," Alisha explained. "During your mission, **you aged only minutes, while the rest of us have aged years.**"

Buzz refused to give up. He blasted off again and again, but fuel crystal after fuel crystal failed. With every flight, everyone on the planet grew older. Alisha married a woman named Kiko and they had a son, Avery. But for Buzz, hardly any time had passed at all.

One day, when Buzz had returned from another failed flight, he went to Alisha's office. But she wasn't there.

"Hi, Buzz," an elderly Alisha said in a holographic message. "I seem to have gone and gotten very old." A little girl wearing a homemade Space Ranger uniform climbed into Alisha's bed.

Alisha introduced the girl as her granddaughter, Izzy. Izzy wanted to be a Space Ranger—just like her grandmother. Then Alisha turned to the camera and told Buzz that she wouldn't be around to see him finish the mission.

Some time later, Buzz's new commander told him that they were **shutting down the hyperspeed fuel program**.

"Commander, I can still do it! I can get us out of here," Buzz protested.

But it was no use. Commander Burnside had made up his mind.

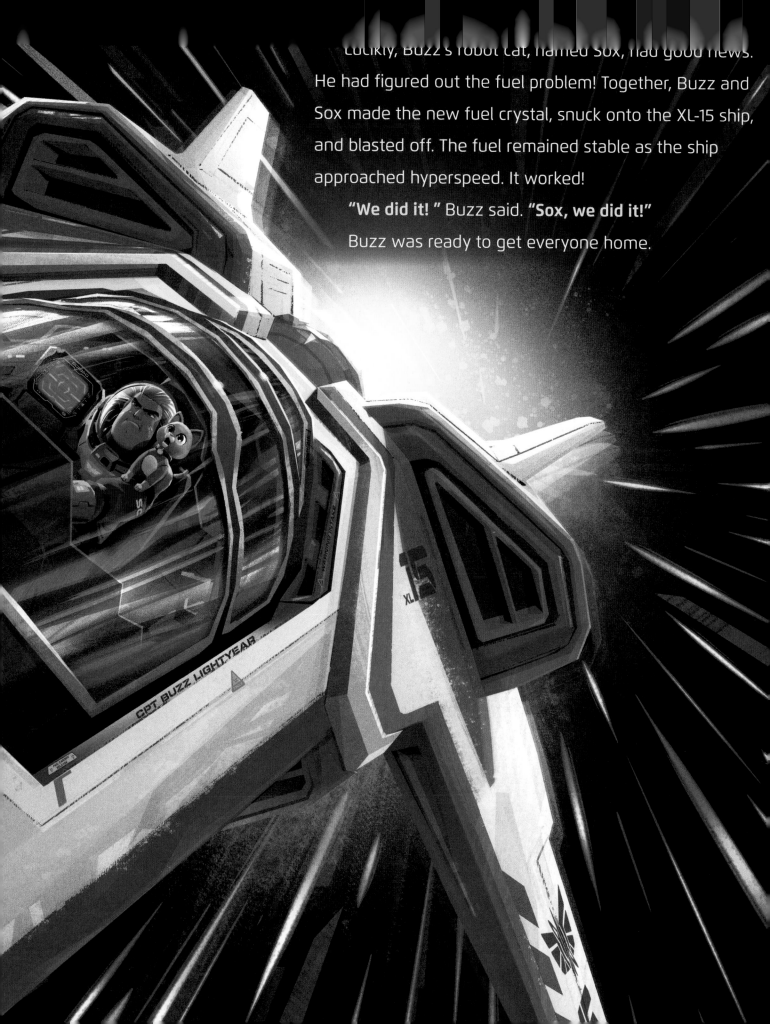

Luckily, Buzz's robot cat, named Sox, had good news.
He had figured out the fuel problem! Together, Buzz and
Sox made the new fuel crystal, snuck onto the XL-15 ship,
and blasted off. The fuel remained stable as the ship
approached hyperspeed. It worked!

"We did it! " Buzz said. **"Sox, we did it!"**

Buzz was ready to get everyone home.

Back on the planet's surface, Buzz opened the cockpit
and hopped out of the spacecraft. Suddenly, someone
pushed him to the ground.

"Shhh!" the mysterious person whispered. "The robots!"

Buzz was stunned to learn that the person was **Alisha's
granddaughter, Izzy**!

Buzz followed Izzy to an outpost, where he met Mo and Darby. They looked like an elite team, ready for anything. But when a robot attacked, Izzy cried, "Fear not! The Junior Zap Patrol has your back!"

Izzy's team did its best to try to stop the robot. But when they failed, Buzz leaped into action and helped them defeat it. In that moment, Buzz realized that Izzy and her team were **just a bunch of rookies.**

With the battle against the robot over, Izzy explained that the Junior Zap Patrol was a team of volunteers who had arrived a week before the robots showed up at the base. The Patrol's mission was to defeat the robots—and their **evil leader, Zurg**!

Buzz realized that taking down Zurg meant he could finally complete his own mission. Although he didn't want to put the rookies in danger, Buzz needed their help to find a ship to take him to Zurg. So the Junior Zap Patrol led him to a storage depot that housed an Armadillo spacecraft.

"Everyone strap in!" Buzz shouted. The Armadillo took off, zooming toward space.

Just then, another ship appeared in the sky and started blasting at the Armadillo. **It was Zurg!**

One of Zurg's blasts hit the Armadillo, and the ship crashed on the dark side of the planet. Before the crew could fix the ship, something blew a hole in the hull! Zurg again! The giant robot reached out his robot claw and said, "Buzz . . . come with me."

Buzz was stunned. **How did this robot know his name?**

Zurg held Buzz up in the air, staring at him with his glowing red eyes. Buzz struggled to break the robot's iron grip, but it was useless. Zurg reached down to a transport disc on his chest and pressed the button. A second later, **he and Buzz were gone!**

Buzz and Zurg reappeared on board a massive ship. It was then that **Zurg revealed his true identity**. **It was Buzz**, but he was much older. This Buzz had also made it to hyperspeed, but Star Command tried to arrest him for stealing the ship. He had escaped and traveled to a **distant future** filled with incredible technology. He'd come back to find Buzz because he had a plan. With the technology of the future and the power of Buzz's fuel crystal, he could change the past. He could travel back to the day they'd crashed the Turnip on T'Kani Prime and **fix their mistake**!

Buzz thought about the offer. If he and this other Buzz changed things so that the Turnip had never crashed, Alisha wouldn't have had her family. They would all be erased! Everything that Alisha and everyone else had worked so hard for would be **gone forever**. **Buzz refused.** Zurg was furious! He extended his robot claw and grabbed Buzz.

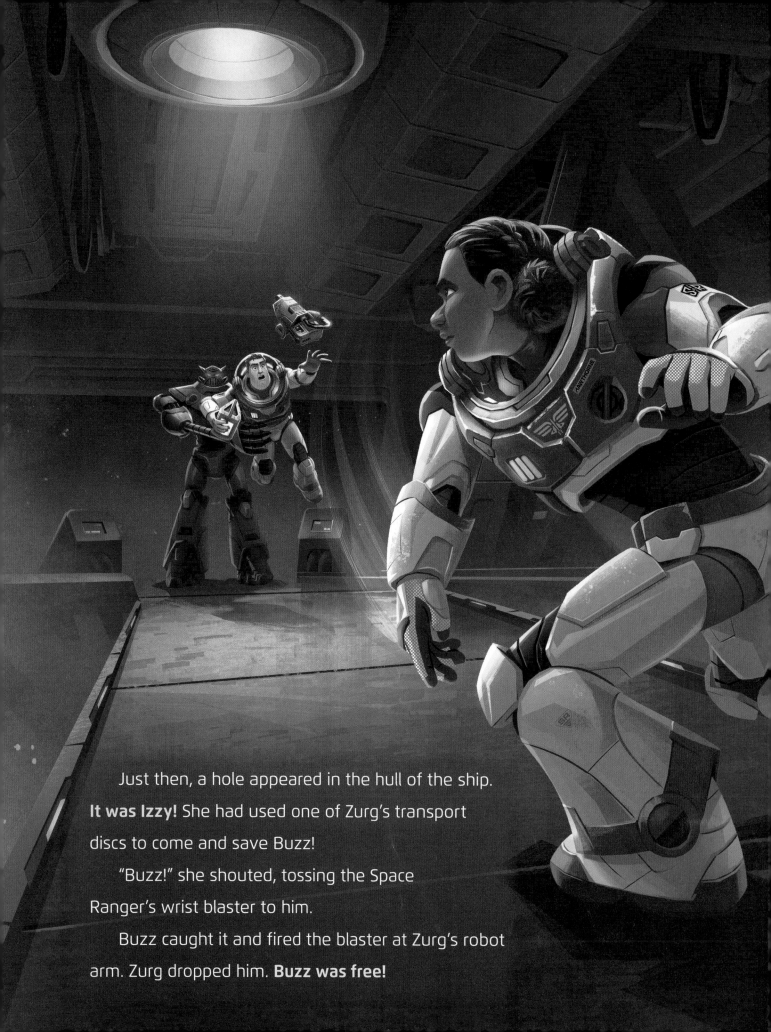

Just then, a hole appeared in the hull of the ship.
It was Izzy! She had used one of Zurg's transport
discs to come and save Buzz!

"Buzz!" she shouted, tossing the Space
Ranger's wrist blaster to him.

Buzz caught it and fired the blaster at Zurg's robot
arm. Zurg dropped him. **Buzz was free!**

The Space Ranger smiled, then blasted the **self-destruct button** on Zurg's ship. The **countdown** started, and after pressing the transport disc, Buzz and Izzy teleported back to the Armadillo.

Buzz ordered Izzy, Sox, Mo, and Darby inside the ship.
Buzz was about to insert the fuel crystal into the Armadillo
when there was a huge explosion. Buzz watched the Armadillo hurtle toward
the planet's surface. **He needed to get to his friends before they crashed!** He
spotted the XL-15 spacecraft and propelled himself toward it, grabbing the side
and pulling himself onto the ship.

Buzz inserted the hyperspeed fuel crystal and climbed into the XL-15's
cockpit.

Then he heard a voice over his comm system say, **"Going somewhere?"**

It was Zurg! He was hanging on to the back of the XL-15!

Buzz knew there was only one thing he could do. He hit the Eject button,
and the seat straps fastened around him. As he blasted out of the XL-15, the
seat became a **jet pack**! Wings extended from his suit, and Buzz flew into
action. He aimed his wrist blaster at the fuel crystal and fired. **The crystal
exploded**, sending Zurg flying through space!

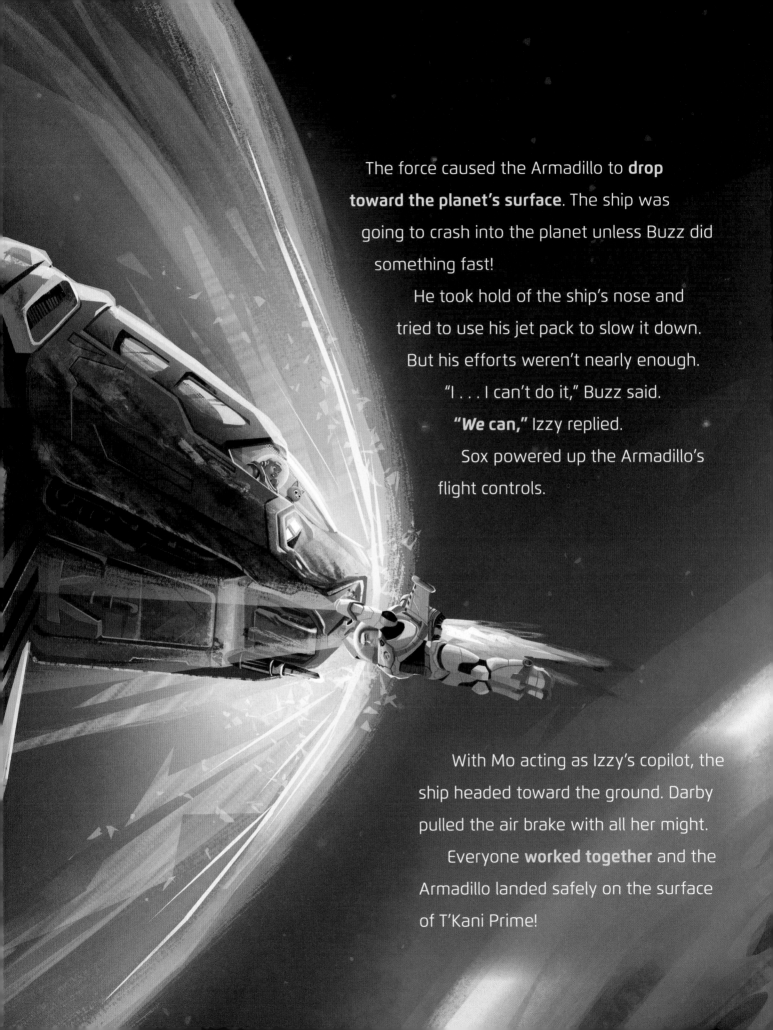

The force caused the Armadillo to **drop toward the planet's surface**. The ship was going to crash into the planet unless Buzz did something fast!

He took hold of the ship's nose and tried to use his jet pack to slow it down. But his efforts weren't nearly enough.

"I . . . I can't do it," Buzz said.

"We can," Izzy replied.

Sox powered up the Armadillo's flight controls.

With Mo acting as Izzy's copilot, the ship headed toward the ground. Darby pulled the air brake with all her might. Everyone **worked together** and the Armadillo landed safely on the surface of T'Kani Prime!

Commander Burnside asked Buzz to start a new version of the Space Ranger Corps—the Universe Protection Division. He could pick his team from Star Command's elite Zap Patrol.

"I already have my team," Buzz said, looking at Izzy, Mo, Darby, and Sox.

Soon the members of the new Universe Protection Division boarded their ship.

While Buzz initiated the launch, Izzy held out a finger toward him. "To infinity . . ." she began.

"And beyond," Buzz finished.